The Great Food Robbery

by Jill Atkins

Illustrated by Seb Burnett

W

FRANKLIN WATTS

First published in 2011 by
Franklin Watts
338 Euston Road
London
NW1 3BH

Franklin Watts Australia
Level 17/207 Kent Street
Sydney
NSW 2000

A CIP catalogue record for this book is available
from the British Library.

ISBN 978 1 4451 0283 2 (hbk)
ISBN 978 1 4451 0289 4 (pbk)

Series Editor: Jackie Hamley
Editor: Melanie Palmer
Series Advisor: Catherine Glavina
Series Designer: Peter Scoulding

Printed in China

Franklin Watts is a division of
Hachette Children's Books,
an Hachette UK company.
www.hachette.co.uk

Robin Rabbit saw
Guzzle and his gang
arrive in town.

Guzzle went into
a baker's shop.

"Give me your bread," he said.

Guzzle went into a butcher's shop.

"Give me your meat," he said.

Guzzle went to the market. "Give me your vegetables," he said.

10

"Guzzle has taken our food," everyone cried.

Guzzle left the town.

Robin followed.

Robin and his friends hid in the trees.

They caught Guzzle!

Robin went back into town ...

CLOSED

20

... and his friends brought all the food back!

Puzzle Time!

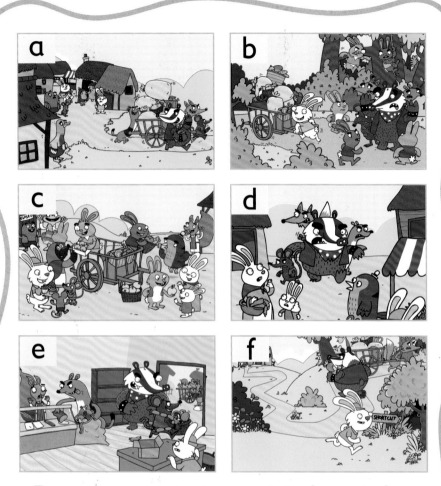

Put these pictures in the right
order and tell the story!

clever

mean

quick

greedy

Which words describe Robin
and which describe Guzzle?

Turn over for answers!

Notes for adults

TADPOLES are structured to provide support for newly independent readers. The stories may also be used by adults for sharing with young children.

Starting to read alone can be daunting. **TADPOLES** help by providing visual support and repeating words and phrases. These books will both develop confidence and encourage reading and rereading for pleasure.

If you are reading this book with a child, here are a few suggestions:

1. Make reading fun! Choose a time to read when you and the child are relaxed and have time to share the story.
2. Talk about the story before you start reading. Look at the cover and the blurb. What might the story be about? Why might the child like it?
3. Encourage the child to retell the story, using the jumbled picture puzzle as a starting point. Extend vocabulary with the matching words to characters puzz
4. Give praise! Remember that small mistakes need not always be corrected.

Answers

Here is the correct order:
1.d 2.e 3.a 4.f 5.b 6.c

Words to describe Robin:
clever, quick

Words to describe Guzzle:
greedy, mean